X Spalding, Maddie.
362.1 Guarding the centers
SPA for disease control and
4/2017 prevention BER

ST. MARY PARISH LIBRARY
FRANKLIN, LOUISIANA

GUARDING
THE CENTERS FOR DISEASE CONTROL AND PREVENTION

BY MADDIE SPALDING

Published by The Child's World®
1980 Lookout Drive • Mankato, MN 56003-1705
800-599-READ • www.childsworld.com

Acknowledgments
The Child's World®: Mary Swensen, Publishing Director
Red Line Editorial: Editorial direction and production
The Design Lab: Design

Design Element: Iaroslav Neliubov/Shutterstock Images
Photographs ©: Douglas C. Pizac/AP Images, cover, 1; LM Otero/AP Images, 5, 20; David Tulis/Atlanta Journal Constitution/AP Images, 6; Shutterstock Images, 10; Katherine Welles/Shutterstock, 12; David Goldman/AP Images, 14; Ric Feld/AP Images, 15; James Gathany/CDC, 17; Juan Carlos Llorca/AP Images, 19

Copyright © 2017 by The Child's World®
All rights reserved. No part of this book may be reproduced or utilized in any form or by any means without written permission from the publisher.

ISBN 9781503808102
LCCN 2015958273

Printed in the United States of America
Mankato, MN
June, 2016
PA02302

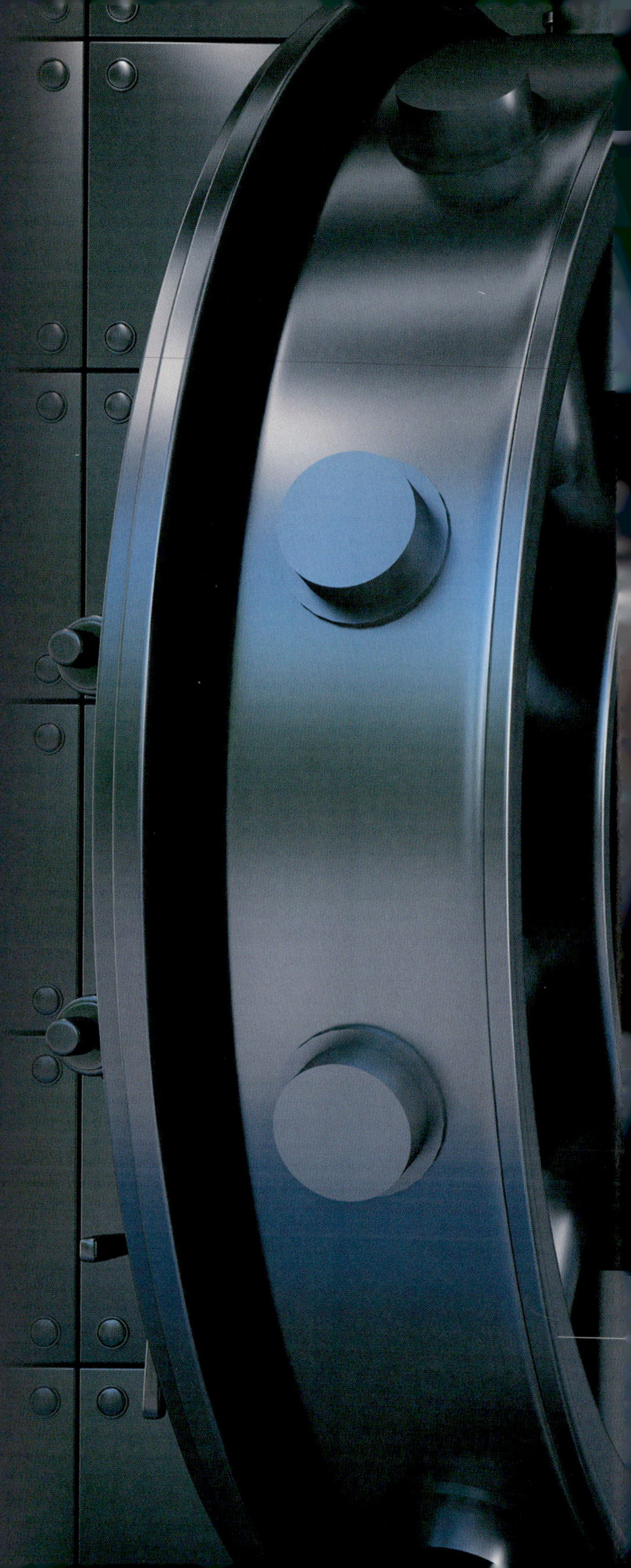

ABOUT THE AUTHOR

Maddie Spalding is an enthusiastic writer and reader. She lives in Minneapolis, Minnesota. Her favorite part of writing is learning about new and interesting subjects.

TABLE OF CONTENTS

CHAPTER 1
Defending against Disease 4

CHAPTER 2
The Birth of the CDC 9

CHAPTER 3
Lab Security................13

CHAPTER 4
Emergency Response.......18

GLOSSARY.........22

TO LEARN MORE 23

INDEX 24

CHAPTER 1

Defending against Disease

Defense can come in many forms. Groups such as the U.S. Army and the Central Intelligence Agency (CIA) work to keep the country safe. They protect citizens against threats from other countries. But all countries face the threat of disease.

The U.S. Centers for Disease Control and Prevention (CDC) defend against this threat. There were more than 50 disease **outbreaks** worldwide in 2015. The CDC worked globally to help manage them.

CDC scientists work in laboratories. They work with **select agents**. These are organisms that can cause diseases. Scientists use select agents to make **vaccines**.

A deadly **virus** threatened the United States in 2014. It was called Ebola. Thomas Eric Duncan

A hazardous material cleaner in Dallas removes an item from an apartment in which an Ebola victim stayed.

CDC director Tom Frieden helped share information during the Ebola scare of 2014.

came to the United States in September. He came from Liberia in West Africa. An Ebola outbreak had hit there. Duncan had helped treat Ebola victims in Liberia. He arrived at the Dallas airport and appeared to be in good health. But Duncan soon showed symptoms of Ebola. He was the first person diagnosed with it on U.S. soil.

News of Duncan's sickness was released. People panicked. Duncan was not treated soon enough. He died. People worried the virus would spread. Many Americans did not know much about the virus. Some thought it spread through the air. They worried there were not enough resources to fight the virus.

The CDC tried to ease the panic. They created better airport security screenings. This way the virus could be caught more quickly. The CDC told medical staff how to treat people with Ebola. The CDC also taught the public about the virus. They explained the virus is rare. They said it cannot be spread through the air.

A few people in the United States did get Ebola. Duncan and one other died. But the virus scare could have turned into an outbreak. The CDC helped make sure it did not.

The CDC also responded to the terrorist attacks on September 11, 2001. Terrorists flew planes into buildings in New York. CDC workers arrived on the scene. They treated injuries and illnesses. Thousands of people lived or worked near the attack site. More than 1,000 of them developed cancer years later. The CDC continued to help them in the following years.

The CDC works with deadly viruses. Labs are placed under high security. This prevents break-ins. It also helps CDC scientists handle select agents carefully. A break-in or mistake could lead to disaster. A deadly outbreak could occur. CDC security makes sure this does not happen.

CDC SECURITY GUIDELINES

The CDC publishes security guidelines. CDC scientists must follow them. Other labs around the country also work with select agents. These labs must follow the rules, too. The guidelines explain how to handle select agents. They also say what equipment to use.

CHAPTER 2

The Birth of the CDC

The CDC fights many diseases. But this was not always the case. The CDC started as the Office of Malaria Control in War Areas (MCWA). The MCWA mainly fought malaria. The disease is carried by some mosquitoes. Malaria symptoms include fever and vomiting. Malaria can result in death if not treated.

The MCWA was created in 1942. American soldiers were fighting in World War II. Many were in the South Pacific. They had to fight in an unfamiliar environment. They faced enemy soldiers. Mosquitoes were another enemy. Mosquitoes live in warm places. The South Pacific has a tropical climate. It was a breeding ground for malaria. American soldiers were infected.

Mosquitoes have long been a danger when it comes to the spread of disease, especially malaria.

Soon soldiers were returning home. Some in the government worried soldiers would spread malaria. Existing antimalarial drugs were not strong enough. The government needed something else to stop the disease from spreading. So they started the MCWA.

The agency formed teams of doctors and scientists. They located people with malaria. They found mosquito breeding grounds. These were often U.S. swamps. They drained these swamps. MCWA members also educated people about malaria. They asked artists to create posters. These posters taught Americans to use good screens in their houses. This would help keep mosquitoes out. Overseas soldiers used bed netting. This kept mosquitoes away at night.

World War II ended in 1945. The MCWA had helped keep Americans healthy. The government wanted to expand the MCWA. They wanted an agency that could fight many more diseases. The agency was renamed in 1946. It was called the Communicable Disease Center. It would later change again to its current name.

The CDC has grown. So have its goals. Malaria was eliminated in the United States in 1951. The CDC still fights malaria in other countries. But its focus has also expanded to

COMMUNICABLE DISEASE CENTER SECURITY

The Communicable Disease Center was in a small building in Atlanta. It occupied one floor. The agency had a limited budget. There were just a few employees. So the building did not have much lab security. But the agency grew. It started working with more dangerous materials. This led to a need for greater safety measures. The CDC headquarters in Atlanta now has state-of-the-art lab security.

Outside the federal CDC headquarters in Atlanta

other health issues. The CDC treats injured and ill people affected by natural disasters. The CDC also makes plans for responding to acts of **bioterrorism**. Bioterrorism can be used to cause illness or death. The CDC continually works on plans to fight such attacks while also treating health issues around the world.

CHAPTER 3

Lab Security

CDC scientists work with **microbes**. Microbes are small select agents. They can only be seen with a microscope. The CDC works with many different microbes. Some do not cause diseases. But other microbes can. Some microbes, such as the Ebola virus, have no approved vaccine.

Microbes are dangerous. Only a few facilities in the country can work with them. The CDC headquarters is one such place. CDC labs are well protected. This keeps workers and the public from becoming infected.

CDC labs are split into groups. Each lab has a **biosafety** level. This level indicates the danger of the microbes in the lab. Biosafety level 1 (BSL-1) labs work with microbes that are not dangerous. Microbes in BSL-2 labs are also often safe. But the microbes in BSL-3 and BSL-4 labs are not. They can be deadly.

Scientists in all labs wear protective clothing. Scientists in BSL-1 labs must wear lab coats and gloves. They often also must wear protective glasses. Scientists in BSL-2 labs wear the same type of clothing. They might also wear face shields.

Scientists in BSL-3 and BSL-4 labs need to wear even more gear. Scientists in BSL-3 labs sometimes

Two microbiologists extract listeria bacteria at the CDC federal headquarters in Atlanta in 2013.

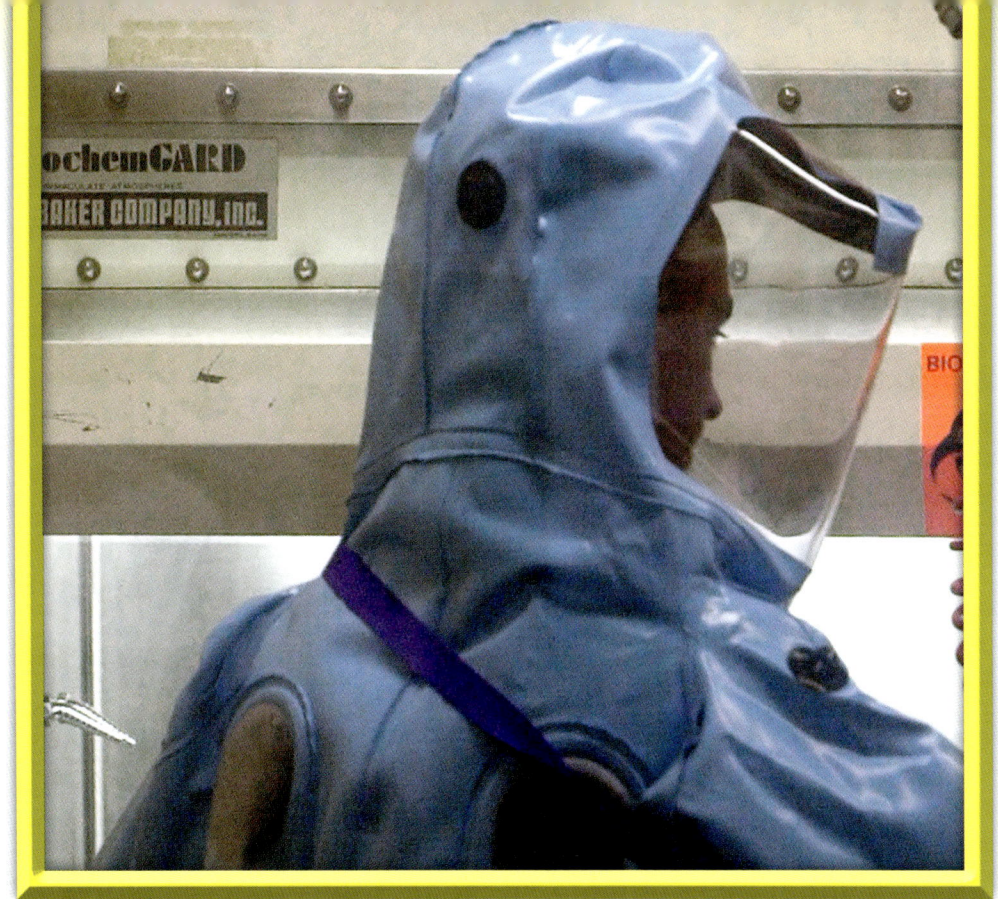
Those working in BSL-4 labs need to be covered from head to toe.

need respirators. These are masks worn over the mouth and nose. The masks keep scientists from breathing in microbes. Scientists in BSL-4 labs wear special full-body suits. There is a hose attached to each suit. This pumps in clean air.

Labs that are BSL-2 or higher have biosafety cabinets. Scientists work with microbes in these cabinets. They protect workers from spills. BSL-2, BSL-3, and BSL-4 labs also have eyewash fountains.

Scientists can get chemicals in their eyes. Eyewash fountains help wash out these chemicals. All labs except for BSL-1 labs have self-closing doors. BSL-4 labs need at least two self-closing doors. These doors keep particles from escaping.

The BSL-4 labs have the highest level of security. The walls of BSL-4 labs are solid concrete. The air pressure is controlled. Clean air is always moving through the labs. This keeps lab air from escaping. A special filter keeps the air clean.

A scientist cannot just walk into a BSL-4 lab. The scientist must first put on scrubs. Scrubs are a type of loose-fitting clothing. Then there is a series of locked doors. These doors are guarded by high-tech equipment. These include eye and fingerprint scanners.

The scientist then puts on a full-body

IRIS SCANNERS

Iris scanners are machines that scan a person's eye. These scanners identify a person from the shape of his or her iris. The iris is the colored part of the eye. Each person has a different iris shape. The U.S. military and the Federal Bureau of Investigation (FBI) also use iris scanners.

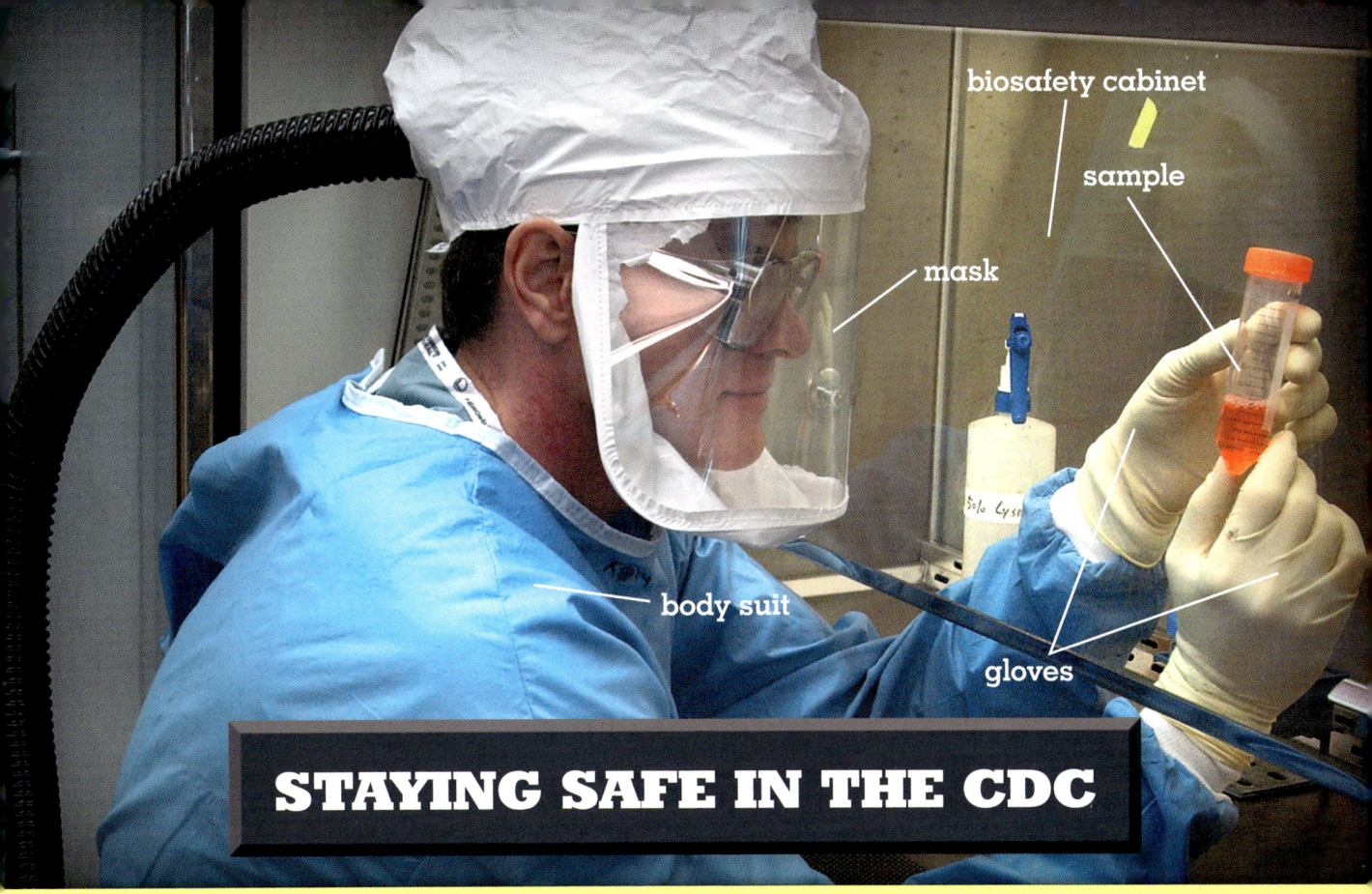

STAYING SAFE IN THE CDC

suit. Then he or she steps into a chemical shower. The suit is sprayed with special chemicals. These kill any viruses. The shower is usually about seven minutes long. The scientist takes another chemical shower after exiting the lab. He or she will also take a regular shower before leaving. These safety measures can be tedious. But they keep viruses from entering or leaving the lab.

CHAPTER 4

Emergency Response

The United States has good resources for fighting diseases. But many tourists visit each year. They could carry a disease with them. It might be one that has never been seen in the country.

Viruses can also **mutate**. They can change and become resistant to vaccines. These are just two reasons why the government needs to be ready for an outbreak. A deadly outbreak is unlikely. But it could happen.

The CDC has detailed plans for handling outbreaks. Part of the plans involve working with state hospitals. The agency tells hospital workers what to do during an outbreak. The CDC has an online network. This lets the CDC communicate quickly with hospitals. Hospitals use this network to tell the CDC about suspected outbreaks.

One of the CDC's most important jobs is teaching others how to deal with disease outbreaks and other biological disasters.

The CDC has a large supply of emergency medicine. This is called the Strategic National Stockpile (SNS). This supply can be used during an outbreak. SNS supplies are kept in secret locations around the country. These supplies can be delivered anywhere in the United States within 12 hours. Hospitals train volunteers to help hand out medicine during an emergency.

Dr. Edward Goodman and other medical professionals were key parts of preventing an Ebola outbreak in 2014.

CDC workers also try to find the cause of the outbreak. They research how it infects people. Some diseases are spread through direct contact with an infected person. Some are spread through animal bites. The CDC will tell the public how the disease spreads. This way people can better avoid the disease.

The CDC will try to separate sick people from healthy people. This is called **quarantine**. Quarantine keeps the disease from spreading. The CDC will treat people in quarantine. There are 20 quarantine stations in the United States. These are located near state borders and airports.

The CDC has plans for many kinds of emergencies. It can respond to disease outbreaks. It is ready to help people after natural disasters. The CDC also knows how to respond to acts of bioterrorism. These emergencies can be scary. But the public can feel safe knowing the CDC is ready to help.

ANTHRAX INCIDENT

The CDC had a minor scare in June 2014. The agency sent bacteria samples to labs on a college campus. It was a bacteria that causes anthrax. Anthrax is an illness that can be deadly. The samples were supposedly safe to handle. So lab workers did not wear protective equipment. But the samples were actually live. The CDC quickly treated the lab workers. No one was infected thanks to the CDC's quick action.

GLOSSARY

biosafety (bye-oh-SAYF-tee) Biosafety is safety relating to biological research. CDC labs have biosafety numbers that indicate the safety measures that should be used in each lab.

bioterrorism (bye-oh-TER-ur-ism) Bioterrorism is the use of a virus or other agent to hurt or kill others. CDC workers are trained to fight bioterrorism.

microbes (MYE-krobes) Microbes are organisms that are too small to be seen without a microscope. CDC scientists have to be careful when studying microbes that are select agents.

mutate (MYOOT-ate) To mutate is to change into something different. Viruses can mutate so that they are resistant to treatment.

outbreaks (OUT-brakes) Outbreaks are a sudden start or increase in something. Disease outbreaks occur when many people suddenly develop a disease.

quarantine (KWOR-uhn-teen) Infected people are placed under quarantine to keep them away from others in an effort to stop a disease from spreading. The CDC might put sick people in quarantine during a disease outbreak.

select agents (si-LEKT AY-juhnts) Select agents are organisms that can cause a disease. The CDC works with select agents in its laboratories.

vaccines (vak-SEENS) Vaccines are treatments that protect against a certain disease. CDC scientists try to create vaccines to prevent diseases.

virus (VYE-ruhss) A virus is a tiny organism that can grow and multiply in living cells. A virus can cause a disease.

TO LEARN MORE

IN THE LIBRARY

Jarrow, Gail. *Fatal Fever: Tracking Down Typhoid Mary*. Honesdale, PA: Calkins Creek, 2015.

Orr, Tamra B. *Tracking an Epidemic*. Ann Arbor, MI: Cherry Lake Publishing, 2014.

Shea, John M. *Viruses Up Close*. New York City: Gareth Stevens Publishing, 2013.

ON THE WEB

Visit our Web site for links about guarding the Centers for Disease Control and Prevention: **childsworld.com/links**

Note to Parents, Teachers, and Librarians: We routinely verify our Web links to make sure they are safe and active sites. So encourage your readers to check them out!

INDEX

Anthrax, 21
Atlanta, 11

bioterrorism, 12

cancer, 8
Central Intelligence Agency (CIA), 4

Dallas, 7
Duncan, Thomas Eric, 4, 6–7

Ebola, 4, 6–7, 13

Federal Bureau of Investigation (FBI), 16

guidelines, 8

laboratories, 4, 8, 13–17
Liberia, 6

malaria, 9–11
mosquitoes, 9–11

Office of Malaria Control in War Areas (MCWA), 9–11

safety gear, 14–17
September 11 attacks, 8
Strategic National Stockpile (SNS), 19

U.S. Army, 4, 9–10

World War II, 9–11